My First Book of

BIBLE ANIMALS

Mark Water

Illustrated by Karen Donnelly

 **VICTOR BOOKS**

A DIVISION OF SCRIPTURE PRESS PUBLICATION INC.
USA CANADA ENGLAND

The Bible is filled with animals of every sort.
This book contains pictures and stories of many Bible animals.
If you want to know more about them, just turn to these
sections of the Bible:

Noah's Ark: *Genesis 6–8*

Jonah's Big Fish: *Book of Jonah*

The Lost Sheep: *Matthew 18:10–14*

Balaam's Donkey: *Numbers 22*

Ant: Proverbs *6:6–8*

Birds: Matthew *6:26*

The Big Search

On the next 16 pages can you find all these *Animals, Birds, People, Places, Numbers* and *Objects*?
When you have found the word, write the page number below.

ANIMALS					
Adders	found on page	Ravens	found on page	100 sheep	found on page
Ants	found on page	Sparrows	found on page	450 feet	found on page
Bears	found on page	Storks	found on page	3,000 camels	found on page
Bees	found on page	**PEOPLE**		6,000 camels	found on page
Camels	found on page	Angel	found on page	**OBJECTS AND OTHER WORDS**	
Cobras	found on page	Balaam	found on page	Ark	found on page
Deer	found on page	Balak	found on page	Beehives	found on page
Donkey	found on page	Ham	found on page	Boat	found on page
Fish	found on page	Japeth	found on page	Chariots	found on page
Gazelle	found on page	Jeremiah	found on page	Cheese	found on page
Goats	found on page	Jesus	found on page	Desert	found on page
Horses	found on page	John		Eyelashes	found on page
Insects	found on page	the Baptist	found on page	Fleeces	found on page
Leopards	found on page	Jonah	found on page	Flock	found on page
Lion	found on page	Noah	found on page	Flood	found on page
Lizards	found on page	Pharisees	found on page	Foot	found on page
Locusts	found on page	Prophet	found on page	Honey	found on page
Reptiles	found on page	Shem	found on page	Milk	found on page
Serpents	found on page	**PLACES**		Olive Leaf	found on page
Sheep	found on page	Israel	found on page	Olive Oil	found on page
Snakes	found on page	Jerusalem	found on page	Parable	found on page
Vipers	found on page	Moab	found on page	Rain	found on page
BIRDS		Ninevah	found on page	Rivers	found on page
Chicks	found on page	Tarshish	found on page	Rocks	found on page
Doves	found on page	**NUMBERS**		Sand	found on page
Eagles	found on page	2 servants	found on page	Shofar	found on page
Eaglet	found on page	5 gallons	found on page	Stables	found on page
Hens	found on page	20 wild animals	found on page	Stick	found on page
Owls	found on page	45 feet	found on page	Stomach	found on page
Quail	found on page	75 feet	found on page	Sword	found on page
		99 sheep	found on page	Tar	found on page

On page 22 *hints* to all the answers are given.

The Floating Zoo

TWO BY TWO
Animals were herded into the ark, two by two: one male animal and one female animal.

People on the Earth had become so evil in Noah's day that God had to act. He told Noah to build a special boat to save his family and all the animals from a terrible flood. God told Noah how to build the ark 450 feet long, 75 feet wide and 45 feet high.

CRAWLING ANIMALS
As well as animals that could walk, Noah collected animals that could only crawl. Your favorite

crawling animal was there, tucked up safely in the ark.

Inside the ark were rooms, stables and nesting-boxes for the animals and birds to live in. There the animals, birds and crawling animals were kept safe from all the rain, the rivers that overflowed and the terrible flood.

COAT OF TAR
The water could not seep through the ark because God had told Noah to paint it with tar on the inside and outside. The great thing about tar is that water cannot get through it.

Noah, with his wife, their three sons, Shem, Ham and Japheth (and their wives), were kept safe in this great floating zoo. This was the first great animal rescue in the world.

IMPORTANT BIRDS
When the flood started to go down, Noah let a raven fly out of the ark. It kept flying around as there was nowhere to land. Then Noah sent out a dove. The water had still not gone down and it flew back to the ark. Seven days later Noah sent out the dove again and it came back with a fresh olive leaf in its beak. After seven more days Noah again sent out the dove. It never returned. Noah knew that it was time to leave the ark.

The Lost Sheep

The top religious men were upset about Jesus being friends with people they thought of as sinners. Jesus told these men a parable to teach them a lesson.

"A shepherd had 100 sheep in his flock. He herded them into the sheepfold to keep them safe. He counted them but there were only 99. The shepherd went into the fields and searched among the rocks until he'd found his missing sheep.

THE MISSING ONE
The shepherd was very worried about his missing sheep. He left his 99 sheep safe and went to look for the missing sheep.

JESUS AND THE SINNERS
The Pharisees were furious that Jesus went and ate meals with so-called sinners.

LOST AND AFRAID
The sheep was stuck between rocks and had cut its leg.

He said to his friends, "I can't tell you how happy I am to have found my lost sheep. Let's celebrate."

Then Jesus said, "Do you understand this story? There is more joy over one sinner that changes his heart than there is for 99 good people who don't need to change."

FIRST AID
The shepherd rubbed in some olive oil to heal the sheep's wounds.

SAFE AT LAST
The shepherd lifted the sheep onto his shoulders and carried him back to the flock.

The Talking Donkey

Balak, king of Moab, had thought up a way to defeat God's people, the Israelites. It wasn't with chariots, or war-camels or an army of soldiers. It was with a curse. King Balak had asked the prophet Balaam to put a curse on the Israelites.

Balaam, with two of his servants, prepared to travel to see Balak. But God sent an angel to stand right in the middle of Balaam's path. Balaam did not see the angel. His two servants did not see the angel. But the donkey clip-clopped off the road into a field to avoid the angel. Balaam hit his faithful donkey with a stick.

AN ANGEL APPEARS
Later God's angel stood on a narrow path that had walls on either side. Again, only the donkey saw him and swerved so close to one of the walls that Balaam's foot was crushed. Balaam hit his faithful donkey again.

AN ANGEL APPEARS AGAIN

The third time the angel stood in Balaam's way the path was so narrow that the donkey could not turn to right or left to avoid the angel. So the faithful donkey did the only thing that was left. She sat down! Balaam, with his throbbing foot, was furious by now, and he reached for his stick again.

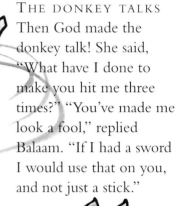

THE DONKEY TALKS

Then God made the donkey talk! She said, "What have I done to make you hit me three times?" "You've made me look a fool," replied Balaam. "If I had a sword I would use that on you, and not just a stick."

ALAAM SEES THE NGEL

hen, at last, the Lord let laam see the angel. The gel was standing in the ad with his sword drawn. hen Balaam bowed face wn to the ground.

Wild Animals

BEAUTIFUL GAZELLES
Another name for deer used in the Bible is gazelle. Gazelles have lovely bodies, large eyes and striking horns.

There are over 20 wild animals mentioned in the Bible. The list includes bears, lions, deer, leopards, goats and sheep. Goats and sheep often grazed together in mixed flocks. Sheep were very important for the Israelites and are talked about 750 times in the Bible.

Jesus said that His followers were like sheep and that He was their Good Shepherd. They hear His voice. He knows them each by name. He calls them and they follow Him. The Good Shepherd fights off thieves who want to kill and steal the sheep.

The Good Shepherd lays down His life for the sheep.

HUNTING BEARS
The light-colored Syrian bear used to roam all over Israel. It hunted sheep and goats.

THE LIONS OF ISRAEL
The lions in Israel were smaller than the African lions and had short curly manes.

CLOTHES FROM SHEEP
Sheep gave wool for clothes. Shepherds wore their fleeces like coats.

THE RAM'S HORN
A ram's horn, the shofar, was blown when hymns praise were sung to God

USEFUL GOATS
Goatskin was used to make tents. Wine and water was kept in goatskin bottles.

A FIERCE FOE
Everyone lived in fear of the powerful, swift leopard. The prophet Jeremiah once warned that "Leopards would tear to pieces anyone who came out of the city."

THE GOOD SHEPHERD
The Good Shepherd looks after his sheep and their lambs, finds them lush green grass and brings back any that have strayed from the flock.

13

The Big Fish

Jonah was God's preacher. God had a tough job for Jonah. "Go to Nineveh," God ordered him, "tell the 120,000 people in Nineveh that I love them." But Jonah did not go to Nineveh. He boarded a boat going in the opposite direction, to Tarshish. He thought he had escaped from God and would not have to do what God wanted.

God sent 10-foot high waves and the boat was about to sink. Jonah told the men that he was running away from God. "So what should we do?" they asked Jonah. He said, "Pick me up, and throw me into the sea. Then it will calm down. It is my fault this great storm has come." Then the men threw Jonah into the sea and it became calm.

GOD'S RESCUE PLAN
Jonah was swallowed. A huge, friendly fish swam right up to Jonah and gulped him down. Jonah stayed in its stomach for three days and nights. While he was there God taught Jonah some lessons.

TRUST IN GOD
Jonah showed his trust in God as he prayed from the fish's stomach.

DRY LAND
Then the Lord spoke to the fish. And the fish coughed and Jonah came out of its stomach onto dry land. Jonah then went off to preach to the people in the wicked town of Nineveh.

15

Birds

The Bible mentions 50 species of birds, and 45 of the Bible books refer to birds, including eagles, owls, storks, quails, sparrows and hens.

STORKS
Storks nested in
the tops of tall
trees.

The Bible says that God cares for His children just as the eagle cares for its young. The parent eagles teach the young eagles, eaglets, to fly by carrying them into the air on their wings and letting them go. If the eaglet gets tired it is taken home to the nest.

Jesus said that even birds which people took no notice of, such as sparrows, were important to God.

LITTLE BIRDS
All different types of small
birds were called sparrows
or "twitterers".

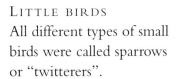

EAGLES
Eagles built their nests on the top of high mountains. The Romans had the eagle as a symbol of their power.

A MOTHER HEN
The mother hen gathers her chicks under her wings. Jesus said that he loved the people of Jerusalem as much as a mother hen loves her chicks.

GOD'S LOVE
Jesus told people to look at the birds and to think what they teach us about God's love.

Reptiles and Insects

Snakes and lizards, and any animals with scales rather than skin or fur, are called reptiles. In the Bible snakes are called adders, cobras, vipers or serpents. One snake, the horned viper, has such a poisonous bite that it can kill within 30 minutes of biting. These horned vipers, although only 18 inches long, move along the ground so quickly that they scare horses.

INSECTS
There are more insects in the world, over one million types or species, than any other kind of animal.

LIZARDS
One of the lizards the Bible, the geck lizard, is the smalle in the world. It ca climb up walls and even walk upside-down on ceilings, because of the stic pads on its feet.

HONEY
Instead of bee hives, people put up pots and hanging baskets so that bees would nest in them. As there was no sugar, honey was a very important food.

ANTS
"Lazy people should learn a lesson from the way ants live. They have no leader, chief or ruler, but they store up their food during the summer getting ready for winter."
Proverbs 6:6–8

LOCUSTS

Locusts, a type of grasshopper, were greatly feared. They arrived in huge swarms, sometimes with over one million locusts in each swarm. They looked like dark clouds, blocking out the sunlight. They were called "destroyers" or "burners of the land", as they gobbled up all the crops. In 15 minutes they could eat all the green leaves, buds and even the bark of a massive tree.

LOCUSTS AND WILD HONEY

The New Testament prophet, John the Baptist, lived on locusts and wild honey.

COBRAS

The Egyptian cobra is poisonous. It has a hood that flares up when it is about to strike. Psalm 58 says that evil people who will not listen to God are like a cobra that will not listen to the snake-charmer's music.

19

Camels

Camels were the trucks of the Bible. If you wanted something heavy carried, especially across deserts, the camel was your animal. If you look at a camel carefully you can see how it was built to travel in the desert.

Its broad feet: they helped the camel to carry its own weight on sand. If camels had thin, pointed feet they would have sunk into the sand at every stride.

Long legs: their long legs meant that their stomachs were far away from the blazing hot sand.

Hump: the single-humped camel of the Bible

CAMELS' HAIR CLOTHES
Camels' hair was woven and made into rough clothes.

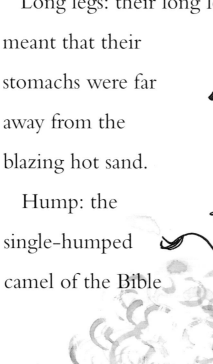

CAMELS AND WAR
Camels were used in wars, especially by the Midianites, as they could run so fast. They traveled at a steady 8-10 miles an hour, and carried large loads.

USES OF A CAMEL
Camels gave milk that was drunk and made into cheese. And cam[el] meat was eaten by Ar[abs]

A SIGN OF WEALTH

In the days of the Old Testament you didn't measure your wealth by banknotes but by the number of animals you owned. Abraham was a very wealthy man and had a great number of camels. Job had 3,000 camels at one time, and at the end of his life he was so rich, and God blessed him so much, that he had 6,000 camels.

carried a reserved tank of food made of fat and muscle. When they had no food to eat, their bodies used this reserve supply of food.

Three stomachs: each of these three stomachs of the camel carried five gallons of water so they could go for up to three days without drinking.

A desert diet: camels thrive on tough plants found in the desert.

The Big Search

Hints to all the answers of your word search

ANIMALS						
Adders	Try page 18 or 19	Ravens	Try page 6 or 7	100 sheep	Try page 8 or 9
Ants	Try page 18 or 19	Sparrows	Try page 16 or 17	450 feet	Try page 6 or 7
Bears	Try page 12 or 13	Storks	Try page 16 or 17	3,000 camels	Try page 20 or 21
Bees	Try page 18 or 19	**PEOPLE**		6,000 camels	Try page 20 or 21
Camels	Try page 10, 11, 20, 21	Angel	Try page 10 or 11	**OBJECTS AND OTHER WORDS**	
Cobras	Try page 18 or 19	Balaam	Try page 10 or 11	Ark	Try page 6 or 7
Deer	Try page 12 or 13	Balak	Try page 10 or 11	Beehives	Try page 18 or 19
Donkey	Try page 10 or 11	Ham	Try page 6 or 7	Boat	Try page 14 or 15
Fish	Try page 14 or 15	Japeth	Try page 6 or 7	Chariots	Try page 10 or 11
Gazelle	Try page 12 or 13	Jeremiah	Try page 12 or 13	Cheese	Try page 20 or 21
Goats	Try page 12 or 13	Jesus	Try page 8, 9, 12, 13, 16 or 17	Desert	Try page 20 or 21
Horses	Try page 18 or 19			Eyelashes	Try page 20 or 21
Insects	Try page 18 or 19	John the Baptist	Try page 18 or 19	Fleeces	Try page 12 or 13
Leopards	Try page 12 or 13	Jonah	Try page 14 or 15	Flock	Try page 8, 9, 12 or 13
Lion	Try page 12 or 13	Noah	Try page 6 or 7		
Lizards	Try page 18 or 19	Pharisees	Try page 8 or 9	Flood	Try page 6 or 7
Locusts	Try page 18 or 19	Prophet	Try page 10, 11, 12 or 13	Foot	Try page 10 or 11
Reptiles	Try page 18 or 19			Honey	Try page 18 or 19
Serpents	Try page 18 or 19	Shem	Try page 6 or 7	Milk	Try page 20 or 21
Sheep	Try page 8, 9, 12 or 13	**PLACES**		Olive Leaf	Try page 6 or 7
		Israel	Try page 12 or 13	Olive Oil	Try page 8 or 9
Snakes	Try page 18 or 19	Jerusalem	Try page 16 or 17	Parable	Try page 8 or 9
Vipers	Try page 18 or 19	Moab	Try page 10 or 11	Rain	Try page 6 or 7
BIRDS		Ninevah	Try page 14 or 15	Rivers	Try page 6 or 7
Chicks	Try page 16 or 17	Tarshish	Try page 14 or 15	Rocks	Try page 8 or 9
Doves	Try page 6 or 7	**NUMBERS**		Sand	Try page 20 or 21
Eagles	Try page 16 or 17	2 servants	Try page 10 or 11	Shofar	Try page 12 or 13
Eaglet	Try page 16 or 17	5 gallons	Try page 20 or 21	Stables	Try page 6 or 7
Hens	Try page 16 or 17	20 wild animals	Try page 12 or 13	Stick	Try page 10 or 11
Owls	Try page 16 or 17	45 feet	Try page 6 or 7	Stomach	Try page 14, 15, 20 or 21
Quail	Try page 16 or 17	75 feet	Try page 6 or 7		
		99 sheep	Try page 8 or 9	Sword	Try page 10 or 11
				Tar	Try page 6 or 7